SOMERSET TALES

Edited By Elle Berry

First published in Great Britain in 2018 by:

 Young**Writers**

Young Writers
Remus House
Coltsfoot Drive
Peterborough
PE2 9BF
Telephone: 01733 890066
Website: www.youngwriters.co.uk

FOREWORD

Young Writers was created in 1991 with the express purpose of promoting and encouraging creative writing. Each competition we create is tailored to the relevant age group, hopefully giving each pupil the inspiration and incentive to create their own piece of work, whether it's a poem or a short story. We truly believe that seeing their work in print gives pupils a sense of achievement and pride.

For Stranger Sagas, we challenged secondary school pupils to write a mini saga – a story in just 100 words. They were given the choice of eight story starters to give their imaginations a kick start:

- "Ouch!"... Instead of blood there were wires...
- "I need to stop," I whisper to myself...
- The mist clears and my name's on the moss-covered gravestone...
- We'd agreed on three meeting places, I'd just reached the last one...
- I remembered his last words: "This is the beginning of the end..."
- They say I'm a traitor...
- A scream echoes outside...
- "You have one chance, choose wisely..."

They could use any one of these to inspire their story, or alternatively they could choose to go it alone and create that all-important story starter themselves. With bizarre beginnings, mysterious middles and enigmatic endings, the resulting tales in this collection cover a range of genres and showcase the talent of the next generation. From fun to frightening to the weird and wonderful, these mini sagas are sure to keep you entertained and take you to strange new worlds.

CONTENTS

Mason Mcphee (12)	63
Juliette Clare Newing (13)	64
Sophie Groom (12)	65
Harvey Fisher (12)	66
Michael John Oliver (13)	67
Artur Vasile (11)	68
Rebecca Hail (12)	69
Jasmine Haines (13)	70
Jessica Longley (12)	71
Oliver Jones-Hawkins (11)	72
James Hewlett (13)	73
Ellie-Grace Newman (13)	74
India Porter (13)	75
Rhys Anderson (12)	76
Lily Evans (12)	77
William Gardner (12)	78
Malachi Crozier (12)	79
Amy Skinner (11)	80
Kevina Williams (11)	81
Teigan Bateman (11)	82
Leon Llewellyn (12)	83
Polly Tottle (12)	84
Bethan Sinclair (12)	85
Ruby Amber-Mae Clements (12)	86
Vibeke Lovise Farnsworth (12)	87
Neve Lacey (11)	88
Joseph Street (11)	89
Andreas Laoutaris (11)	90
Madison James (13)	91
Jacob Porter (12)	92
Thomas Walter (13)	93
Poppy Kilduff (11)	94
Aleisha Baker (12)	95
Niamh Madeline Criddle (13)	96
Scarlett Morris (12)	97
Samantha Fisher (12)	98
Jack Richardson (11)	99
Rosetta Luxon (12)	100
Kamil Gabriel Majdczak (13)	101
Morgan Fear (11)	102
Bradley Waite (11)	103
Lauren Summer Lewis (13)	104
Liam Burrow (12)	105

Elliot Harris (13)	106
Millie Jones (12)	107
Joseph Fitzpatrick (11)	108
Amy Denvir (11)	109
Zak Lewis (12)	110
Leo Durrant (11)	111
Sophie Chislett (12)	112
Tegan Louise Kelleher (11)	113
Alessandro Salamanca (11)	114
Callum Sinnett Priestley (13)	115
Kyle Higgs (12)	116
Christian William Whyte (12)	117
Harley Buncombe (11)	118
Louis Clarke (12)	119
Sienna Field (13)	120
Rory Kerton (12)	121
Oakley Jai Timms (12)	122
Korben Phillip Thomas Noble (11)	123
Mackenzie Crook (12)	124
Freddie Hatchard (12)	125
Archy Ferguson (12)	126
Grace Reading (12)	127

Kings Of Wessex Academy, Cheddar

Archie Waymouth (14)	128
David Warren King (14)	129
Lydia Menear (13)	130
Erin Hemms (14)	131
Kell Gardner (14)	132
Abigail Campbell (14)	133
Sophie Angell (14)	134
Rachel Stockley (16)	135
Natasha Stewart (14)	136
Jemima Beatrice Ryles (13)	137

St Dunstan's School, Glastonbury

Jack Crosweller (14)	138
James Manley (11)	139
Ruby Warwick Brown (13)	140
Finlay Daniel Joseph Milton (12)	141

Corey Pople (12)	142
Chantelle Aston (13)	143
Drew Stone (13)	144
Megan Curtis (14)	145
Aurelia Thyer (11)	146
Shaylah Howarth (14)	147
Anwyn Johnson (14)	148
Corey Howe (14)	149
Jacob Millard (13)	150
Will Porter (14)	151
Youssef Louzi (13)	152
Emillie Marshfield (14)	153
Trixie Hargood (14)	154
Leon Sparks (14)	155
Jasmine Sheppard (11)	156

Westfield Academy, Yeovil

Brandon MJ Evans (14)	157
Gemma Godfrey (15)	158
James Matthews (16)	159
Wiktoria Hajduk (12)	160
Megan Cait Christopher (16)	161
Eva Short (11)	162

THE MINI SAGAS

You Choose

They say I'm a traitor. I didn't know what they meant until today... I awoke from a coma three days ago. I have no recollection of who I am, where I came from. The doctors asked me to write up an account of my life, but the problem is that I don't even know myself!

Suddenly, in my mind I can see a man. He is holding matches in one hand and something round and deadly in the other. I realise that there is a gun on the floor in front of me! I have a choice. Gun or bomb?

Poppy Holt

A Little Broken

"I need to stop," I whispered to myself, voice quivering. My inadequate body slid down a wall, a sea of salty tears came crashing down my face. The harsh wind blew like miniscule shards of glass.

I looked down at my slim body. It was small and feeble, shaking like a leaf on a tree. Loathsome thoughts flooded my mind, nothing a little girl should imagine; little grating murmurs, whispering the most repulsive things. "Worthless." "Loner." "Freak."

I had to stop running from my problems because this wasn't healthy. But I guessed everyone was a little broken inside at times.

Rebecca Scanlon (14)
Bridgwater College Academy, Bridgwater

The Game

We'd agreed on three meeting places. I'd just reached the last one... silence. "The first challenge awaits," echoed through the walls of the stadium that overlooked its prey. It fed off... *fear!* Nothing but darkness, but the light was flickering inside me.

My colleagues were nowhere to be seen. Well, I could not see, it was like being blind. I felt hopeless. Scared... But I couldn't be, because it could see me, staring at every emotion. Every movement I made, it got stronger and stronger and... "Go further if you dare." The deafening sound once again! It sickened me.

Emily Pearson (14)
Bridgwater College Academy, Bridgwater

The Great Bombardment

I remembered his last words: "This is the beginning of the end," as I ran for my life, dodging power-fillet pellets that struck the ground. Feeling I was being toyed with, I would reach the brink of safety before being struck by a mass of falling rock.

Miniscule stones soon progressed into large pebbles. My motivation? To reach my beloved wife, wishing not to finish like my friend before me.

My hope dwindled, the onslaught continued, my legs tore from constant running. Would I survive to see through this? The gargantuan shadow cast around me confirmed my horrific suspicions...

Toby Epps (14)

Bridgwater College Academy, Bridgwater

The Unknown Story

"Ouch!" instead of blood there were wires. I thought I was human! What was I?

Shivers rushed down my spine like a current of electricity. The blood-curdling truth was revealed in shock. I gasped for air. *Bang!* I suddenly heard a loud thud behind me. I dashed, leaving the haunted horror house in the distance, getting smaller and smaller until it vanished.

I jumped into a tree and heard it again. I suddenly turned around in fear, my whole body was shaking. I felt like I was being watched with my every move. I felt like eyes were everywhere. "Argh!"

Holly James (13)
Bridgwater College Academy, Bridgwater

The Everlasting Candles

I remembered his last words, "This is the beginning of the end."

As I knelt on the mossy ground, I'd given up everything for this candle. Now I had to destroy it and beg in mercy for my own life.

This was the candle that turned me into a monster, turned me against everything I loved.

I threw it with passion into the well of wisdom, however it kept burning.

I slowly stepped towards the well without doing anything.

"Not again!" I screamed as I trembled face-first into the well.

This was my loss of dignity.

Callum Renton (14)
Bridgwater College Academy, Bridgwater

Betrayal

A scream echoed, the cold shivered down my spine. The flickering light reflected on my face as the warm breeze of the building engulfed my body.

I pushed open the creaky, metal door and was greeted by a dirty, derelict reception room.

I locked the door and sat against it, tears ran down my cheeks as images of her limp body flooded into my mind, his gun against her head.

Wiping the tears away, I peered out of the window. There he stood, gun pointing my way.

They said I was the traitor. They couldn't have been more wrong.

Jessica Legg (13)
Bridgwater College Academy, Bridgwater

The Beginning Of The End

I remembered his last words: "This is the beginning of the end," bleeding out as he was trying to catch a breath. I could barely hear him as thousands of bullets were penetrating the sky. Unfortunately, he wasn't the only one, many others lost their lives, landing either in No Man's Land or dirty trenches filled with rats and bullet shells. People were screaming in terror as fifty gas bombs were fired at us. Those who had masks were safe. Those who didn't, died. I saw people choking and drowning in their own blood.

Jan Tabola (14)
Bridgwater College Academy, Bridgwater

Traitor

They said I was a traitor but I wasn't, it was an accident, I really didn't mean for this to ever happen. It was the worst feeling, everyone saying how sorry they were for my loss, and it was my fault! I wished I'd never gone out, I wished I'd never seen him that night and I wished I'd just walked away when he was saying all those horrible things. Even if he had said all those horrible things, I never, ever should have done what I did. I shouldn't have done it.

It would haunt me, every day, forever.

Aimee Masters (14)
Bridgwater College Academy, Bridgwater

Meeting Death

"I need to stop!" I whispered to myself through a forceful trance. Losing control, I unwillingly squelched into the mist, approaching anyone's dreaded fear, the haunted mansion! Cherished memories faded, the light in my eyes dimmed. Suddenly, the colossal door creaked dauntingly - I was inside!

My mind blocked, holding a blade, I walked. Palms sweating, my hands rose as overwhelming memories flooded back. There were blood-curdling screams and something dripped from my head. Held by an unbreakable grip, crying out, losing breath, I struggled for freedom.

Next, my mind a hurricane, I sat up feebly, remembering the traumatising nightmare.

Evie Mai Jones (11)
King Alfred School, Highbridge

Personalities

"What do you mean I only have one chance?" oozed Bob.

"Because there is a life or death question I'm going to ask you," mumbled Jimmy.

"Go on then!" exclaimed Bob.

"You have three choices, come with me and rule the world, be a normal kid, or fight me," whispered Jimmy.

"Umm," whimpered Bob.

"Answer me now Bob, or you will just die now!" shouted Jimmy.

"Okay, okay!"

"Yes?"

"I choose to fight you on the spot and get you out of my mind!"

"Bad choice Bob, because I will kill you on the spot, little Bobby!"

Brandon Clark Fear (12)
King Alfred School, Highbridge

Strangest Of Places...

"You have one chance, choose wisely," I kept repeating to myself.

Today, I would escape from all these experiments, just because I was some 'superhero'. I wasn't... I had telekinesis. When they weren't looking I ran frantically out the door. I got all the way to the end of the field and... no! There was an electric fence. 'K.e.e.p. O.u.t. *Danger!*'

Oh no, what should I do?

I realised there was soft soil beneath me. I dug and was free!

Hold on, what was that?... "Willow, you can't hide from me!" I freaked. *Crunch* went the bones. "Hehe, whoops!"

Gracie Wilson (11)
King Alfred School, Highbridge

The Bloodstained Girl!

"I need to stop," I whispered to myself. Just then, we stopped.

"What's that in the distance?" John asked.

Suddenly, there were people in the distance. They were wearing rags.

Richard started puffing harder on his cigarette.

"Richard, slow down, you're gonna give yourself a heart attack," I shouted.

"Can you guys see that, or is it just me?" John barked.

Just then, there was a little girl staring at us. She was wearing a white dress. She had blood stains on her dress.

All of a sudden, the ground started to shake! Where was the girl and her family?

Emily Forey (11)
King Alfred School, Highbridge

The Sinner Exterminator

... spoke the deep, mysterious voice from the other side of the phone. "Give me the name of a sinner to die or your sister is next!" I started panicking, all I could hear was my clock churning in the background. *Tick-tock.*

"Why are you doing this to me? Why me?" I shouted into my phone. A tear rolled down my face.

"Pick a name! Now!" blasted the voice, echoing through my head.

"I... I don't know, please don't hurt her!" I begged.

"Pick now Betty!"

"Okay, I pick Nick Lewis!"

"Good! I knew you were a bad girl!"

Danielle Karen Scott (13)
King Alfred School, Highbridge

The Accidental Hero

"You have one chance, choose wisely..." said the man.

"1979," said George.

Bang! Suddenly, he was there. He went over to an entrance to a door, recognising John Lennon. He went over with one of his singles, Imagine. He said, "Can I have your autograph?"

John put, 'To George.'

"Thank you," said George.

Later that day, he saw a man in the shadows. John and Yoko walked to the entrance and the man in the shadows shot him.

George jumped in front of the gun, taking the only bullet. John was surprised and George was transported back to 2020.

Matthew Ethridge (11)
King Alfred School, Highbridge

Unknown

They say I'm a traitor.
Clock ticking.
But that's exaggeration.
Tick-tock.
Walking out into the open space.
Tick-tock.
The moonlight projects down on me and my opponent.
Time is up. It's a showdown.
The stares are of pure death. In a moment, one will be victorious. The other dead on the hard concrete.
My mum told me I'd be victorious, but not like this.
My heart racing, needing more oxygen to help me cope. I can't lie, I am terrified.
He pulls his gun at me. I gulp. Still not knowing who he is, I pull out mine...

Charlotte Richer (13)

King Alfred School, Highbridge

The Diary Of The Dead Man

They said I was a traitor...

... but they didn't know nothing.

The pearly white moon glazed through cracks, illuminating the cave. The night's glaze snarled, the moon slowly faded away. This life shouldn't have been lived by anyone. The relentless struggling person. I didn't want anything to happen.

The day this occurred, all chaos broke loose. They chained me, crimson blood poured from the ghastly wounds I got given by the whip that stroked my back with a *crack*.

I escaped and ran. For the last three weeks, I'd been hiding in solitary. It was funny how a human becoming an animal sometimes survived.

Sam Marsh (13)

King Alfred School, Highbridge

The Mist Cleared And My Name Was On The Moss-Covered Gravestone

"I don't understand," I mumbled. The death date on the stone was dated yesterday. How could that be?
Then, all of a sudden, I heard a voice from the woods!
"Come here, I've waited too long!" I was frozen with fear.
"There's an empty coffin, it needs to be filled."
His voice grew louder, "My knife isn't blood stained."
My brain wasn't moving but I'd never run so fast. I couldn't tell which way I was running. I was either running to the A-road or into the woods. I was going to see light eventually, whichever way I ran.

Will Dyer (13)
King Alfred School, Highbridge

The Mysterious Death

I only had one chance to choose wisely... good or evil? My secret was out, they knew now. Ricky had sussed me out. Standing there trembling, the electric fence standing over my head, I heard a huge rustle.

"What does this mean?" I said while shivering.

"You are not alone Christopher," said a shallow voice from behind.

"What? Who's there?"

Five seconds before I knew it, I was being dragged through sharp objects, it was like piercing knives. He dragged me under the lethal electric fence, it was like I had been in a cat fight. It was the end...

Tanya Berry (12)
King Alfred School, Highbridge

Cold Feet

The mist clears and my name's on the moss-covered gravestone. "Argh!" I scream and turn around. I can't bear to keep staring at my grave.

As soon as my frozen, pale, scared face turns around, I see a dark red, frightening sign which reads, 'You weren't meant to see this, now you're stuck here.'

Thick stone walls emerge out of the ground right beside me. I try to make a run for it, but the walls rise up to the sky even quicker. I scream for help but I can't speak.

Suddenly, a loud phone alarm starts to ring... *ding-a-ling-a-ling!*

Luke Baker (12)

King Alfred School, Highbridge

The Bin

We'd agreed on three meeting places. I'd just reached the last one, the arcade, the others were the woods next to Noah's house and the school grounds. I tried to reach them through the walkie-talkie but I couldn't get a signal.

Suddenly, I heard a rattling, like something was stuck. It was coming from the bin behind the arcade. As I hesitated to walk over, it suddenly stopped.

A couple of seconds passed, then suddenly it started rattling louder and more violently than before.

I grabbed a nearby broom as I charged at it. I opened it...
"Oh my...!"

Lomond Bradley (12)
King Alfred School, Highbridge

Nazi-Orden

"You have one choice, choose wisely," whispered Bojangles, the German president.

Joey, an English soldier who'd been captured, had a little think about his decision. He didn't know what to pick. He could either die or go with the Nazis. He knew if he went to the Nazis he'd be betraying the English and he would feel guilty. He wanted to survive.

He looked around and took in everything he had accomplished in life and all the friends he had, and how much his parents cared for him.

He said, "Goodbye cruel world. I love you so much, Mum, Dad."

Daniel Hughes (11)
King Alfred School, Highbridge

The Victim

"I need to stop," I whispered to myself as I slowly lowered the sharp piece of glass to the ground, letting the victim leave without a single scratch. It was a dark, gloomy night, I couldn't see anything as my eyes wouldn't adjust to the light. Breathing heavily... heart racing... mind baffled, I couldn't help myself, the crimes were getting worse as I remembered my sorrowful past. Tears rolled down my cheeks. I realised my mistake. "What have I become?" As the words kept playing in my head I wondered, *why am I like this?* What had become of me?

Halle Jade Gordon-Smith (11)
King Alfred School, Highbridge

Bound To The End

We'd agreed on three meeting places. I'd just reached the last one.
As I drove up onto the shambolic driveway, I felt the adrenaline pound through me. Was it the right place and time?
The wheels of the deep-rooted car screeched with the rustle of gravel. I got out in a daze, this was more than I was expecting. My polished shoes touched the crunch of autumn leaves scattered on the dry dust. Behind this almighty asset, was the midnight sky, full of shining stars. My head filled with dark worries. Then, unexpectedly, a ghastly silhouette appeared. The pace quickened...

Alicia Slade (11)
King Alfred School, Highbridge

Why Me?

"I need to stop," I whispered to myself, trying not to eat all of the food. But I hadn't eaten in five days though. I only got food every five days and I had been down here for three months.

"I need to find a way out, if there's a way in, there's a way out," I said desperately to myself. *What I could have done to deserve this torment?* I kept thinking.

"You know what you have done," said a voice coming from the shadows.

"Maybe, but why you? I trusted you," I replied.

"You are a mass murderer."

Rubi-Mae Heyward (12)
King Alfred School, Highbridge

Running From Truth

What was I doing? Something intolerable was tormenting my brain. Something told me to run, *run!*

Following it, running every millisecond, I turned around to peep over my shoulder. More petrified than ever, I anticipated what could come next. It was like the moonlight was leading my path, flooding the forest with light, the connection grew stronger. It led me to the graveyard. There was a body lying there, was it alive?

I gingerly crept towards the body, the brains oozed out of the ears. I moved the hair that was draped over the lifeless face. The body was mine...

Poppy Almaz Scarlett Dinham (12)
King Alfred School, Highbridge

Cliff Jump

"You have one chance, choose wisely..." This was racing through my head; *bottle it or throttle it*. I rode towards the cliff. I jumped and throttled her over the cliff edge. What now?

A face appeared. The cliff grew. A person was emerging. A monstrosity of a man was approaching! As quick as lightning, a hand was before me.

An escape route, a perfectly angled ramp to ride up. Should I risk it? Oh yes; I remembered my speed gauge told me the future. *Let's do this, girl.*

I rode up the ramp, hand closing. My future hadn't been told...

Jacob Radford (11)
King Alfred School, Highbridge

The Full Moon

A scream echoed outside...

... I knew I had to run.

Another scream, closer. That could be Lucy. It could be me next... "Okay, think Ange," I looked up - "that's it!" There was a rope hanging down; I was a good climber. I grabbed it. *Bang!* It came from above, "Dang it." The crash was deafening! In a shower of dust and splinters, a mass of fur and claws landed, scrabbling on the straw-covered floor. The stench was overwhelming. I was transfixed.

I knew the moment I broke eye contact would be the moment it sunk its bloodied jaws into my pulsing throat...

Izzy Thomas (12)
King Alfred School, Highbridge

The Scream...

I look up to the midnight sky and I can hear the crickets chirping in the grass. "No," I say, "I can't go back." I stare at the house. Broken windows. Spider webs. Rain plunges into the soggy grass.
I pull open the massive door and trudge into the unlit hallway. Something isn't right... but I keep walking.
I look around to the draughty window. As I walk up the stairs, I hear a slight echo of footsteps. I realise it's just my head and keep going.
Just then, a high-pitched scream echoes from downstairs and the door slams shut...

Caitlin Hopkins (13)
King Alfred School, Highbridge

The Time I Said Goodbye

A scream echoed, it was from inside the house... Mum was in pain. The cancer had gotten to her heart. She was extremely weak and only had one month to live. What had our lives come to? Christmas was around the corner, a special time to us. "We can't lose her before Christmas, it would never be the same without her. She's the bubbly light in the family that makes our lives good."

"Shelley, are you okay?" my nan said as my mum rapidly fell...

She was dead.

I emotionally fell to the floor. My life was awfully ripped apart.

Keira Palmer (11)
King Alfred School, Highbridge

Innocent

They say I'm a traitor, but they know I'm not. I've been here for several days, feels like more. Every day a random piece of junk walks past my cell; silly AI creatures. Nothing new ever happens until I have my check-up, more like hell, I still feel the pain. My cell isn't what you'd call fun, random poem books for five-year-olds. However, my day could get worse. My check-up robot is here, not holding his usual object, holding a... knife?

My time is over, if anyone finds this, tell my family about me. I'm innocent, believe me, please...

Samuel Olbrechts (12)

King Alfred School, Highbridge

I Saved Them

They said I was a traitor. They said I'd failed them. No! It couldn't be my fault, right? No, no, no. It was impossible. The Hook Man came after us with his rusty, sharp hook. They said he slaughtered many people. He killed my friends! I couldn't save them.

No. The voices. They were still here. They whispered unspoken curses that would terrify the most evil monsters. I glanced at my reflection in the window. I saw their bodies. I saw their ghosts. They pointed at me with death in their eyes. They pointed, "It will always be your fault."

Dominic Mylett-Haddley (13)
King Alfred School, Highbridge

Midnight Kidnapper

"You have one chance, choose wisely." It's either I die or my family dies.

I look at my family, pale and terrified. I then look at the murderer, a psychopathic smile creeping on his face. He asks me the question again but even louder. I'm trapped... I can't escape... I'm tied to a chair. "Ouch!" A blinding pain comes to me, blood trickles down my temple and drips on the floor. *Drip... drip... drip...*

I scream with anger and pain because I've come to realise the troubling truth... No one will survive tonight...

Kyra Gabrielle Wade (12)
King Alfred School, Highbridge

Beginning Of The End

I remembered his last words: "This is the beginning of the end." What was meant by that? Then I saw pictures, images that I'd never seen before in my entire life. The images were made from the mist when he disappeared; it was swirling around like it was trying to signal something to me. What I didn't understand was whether it was dangerous, was it outstanding or was I overthinking the images that I was seeing?

Staring like I was looking through a soul, the mist dropped and shattered like glass. Something grabbed me into a mysterious black hole.

Jessica Tudor (12)
King Alfred School, Highbridge

The End Of The Beginning

"You have one chance, choose wisely..." That was the final thing I heard before I came here. And I didn't know how I'd gotten here. I was terrified and I heard echoing footsteps and breathing. I was shaking like a motor when it was on. The footsteps were getting closer and I couldn't find my way out of here.

Day thirteen. A scream echoed outside. I thought I was done, having escaped the thing yesterday but only narrowly. I didn't know what it was. I was scared. It was coming for me. It was here.

Please someone, send help!

Joseph Lynch (11)
King Alfred School, Highbridge

The Beginning Of Danger

I remembered his last words: "This is the beginning of the end..."

An unforgettable past dawned on me as I remembered. I was walking through the forest with bloodshot eyes. *Crunch!* As I turned around, the darkness engulfed me when I saw his face. Pale like a vampire, smiling like a clown.

I ran, my body aching all over, my heart racing. I dropped. He drew nearer.

I picked up the nearest piece of wood, shivering, I hit him. Blood gushed out of his head. He stared at me, creepily. He screamed an ear-piercing scream. What had I done?

Molly Nolan Kendrew (12)
King Alfred School, Highbridge

Curse From A Key

"You have one chance, choose wisely," said the evil genie who was keeping me hostage aboard his golden lamp ship. "You can either give me the key and I let you go or you don't give me the key, stay aboard the ship and work as my slave forever! Bearing in mind you would have to give me £1000 as a payment for letting you stay aboard my ship and for feeding you glop once a day."

"What?" I blurted out after he said this.

"So, what will it be? My prisoner, freedom or captivity?" the nasty, golden genie said...

Libby Eatwell (12)
King Alfred School, Highbridge

The Hotel Down The Alley

The mist cleared and my name was on the moss-covered gravestone outside Hotel Doom And Gloom. I was with my brother, sister, mum and dad for a weekend out.

As I entered, the floorboards squeaked and groaned and the door slammed shut. The wind picked up and the only sound was the sound of the autumn leaves rustling around outside, getting dragged up by Storm Emma.

"Hello, I would like to sign up. *Hello, can you hear me*?" Mum yelled.

Behind the desk was a painting with real life brown plaits. I recognised her, like she was... me...

Poppy Groves (11)
King Alfred School, Highbridge

A Bloody Mess

Everything went quiet, the jet-black crows evaporated into thin air. No one was in sight. As I approached the rigid and obscure gravestone, a crystal figure appeared, holding a jagged, bloody scythe. It whispered as it approached, then it bellowed, shouting at the top of its voice. My ears bled and my eyes stung. I began to run, faster and faster, quicker and quicker. I didn't get anywhere.

It seemed that the mist was coming back. I was trapped... it crept closer and closer, when its scythe penetrated my soul. I fell to my knees, broken, destroyed, hurt.

Mark Staite (12)
King Alfred School, Highbridge

The Kidnap

We'd agreed on three meeting places, I'd just reached the final one.

As I waited, breathless, for Flynn to turn up, a million thoughts were racing through my head. All of a sudden, I heard my name, "Izzy, Izzy..." It echoed through the woods. I wandered towards the voice.

Unexpectedly, a dirty, muddy hand grabbed my wrist and I was dragged backwards through a bush. As I came face-to-face with a scruffy, old man, I let out a blood-curdling scream. He shoved his hand over my mouth, cutting off my breath. I thought I was going to die...

Lyla Pike (12)
King Alfred School, Highbridge

The Shadows

"It's very rare, mistakes happen! What could be so valuable about it anyway?" I said adamantly. I put my hands in my pockets and continued to plod home. I hesitated, should I even glance at it?

When I arrived home, I ran upstairs, grabbed the sheet from my pocket and began to read. My face instantly went white. My heart froze. This was why it was so valuable!

Pressure began to build. I tore the paper in half before anything could happen. I was too late. Three dark shadows appeared and whisked around me. "Forgive me!" I pleaded.

Katie May Bell (12)
King Alfred School, Highbridge

Never Meet Strangers

A scream echoed outside but I swore this was the place he said I needed to meet at. A shiver ran down my spine, remembering all the words our teacher had told us, "Never meet strangers!"

Slowly, I walked up to the door. A shadow walked past, the blinds swayed, the door knob started to turn. *Creak, crack, crunch*, a man stood there with a smile, cheek to cheek. "Come in, come in." I slowly walked in, step by step.

As I walked around, I saw blood spattered on walls, dead bodies surrounded me, a bloody hand grabbed my neck...

Isabelle Mae Puddy (11)

King Alfred School, Highbridge

'Found You'

As his legs buckled, his limp body fell to the floor. I didn't want to leave him, but I couldn't stop. Adrenaline kicked in as I powered through the never-ending maze, a blood-curdling scream echoed throughout. My hair stood up as I ran, dodging and turning as sweat trickled down my head. I heard another scream, this time closer. My head was thumping. I suddenly stopped as my neck jolted. His hands wrapped around my ankle. I'd never forget his widened pupils and pale face. His arms thumped to the ground. He was dead... "I found you!"

Mya Carey (12)
King Alfred School, Highbridge

Sector 347: Escape

Razor-sharp talons slashed and scraped at my chest. In a desperate attempt to survive, I jolted forward and penetrated the heart of the machine. Acidic fluids in the colour of shining emerald dripped from my target.

Free from my chains, I stumbled down a dark corridor surrounded by crimson, flashing lights and ear-piercing sirens. Confused and exhausted, I saw a faint light at the end of the corridor and crawled towards it. It seemed to get closer, yet seemed so far away as the darkness began to weigh on me.

I might never make it, crawling there...

Harrison Garland (13)
King Alfred School, Highbridge

I Still See You

I had a party with my friends, Tom brought a Ouija board. We played at midnight, nothing happened! So we put it away.

Two days later, I was watching television with Mum and Dad, and suddenly we had a power cut. Then the phone rang and a dark voice said while laughing, "I can see you!" Mum and Dad closed the blinds and he said it again, "I can see you!"

Dad said, "Get in the cupboard."

Mum followed, then Dad. Suddenly, the phone call ended. Then it happened again and a mysterious, scary man jumped onto us...

Mackenzie Hudghton (11)
King Alfred School, Highbridge

Knock, Knock

"I need to stop," I whispered to myself as I carried on playing with my doll. A strange feeling came over me that day, I could sense something was going to happen, I just couldn't quite tell what.

Knock, knock... my doll was gone.

I thought nothing of it as I was a paranormal person anyway so I turned away and went back to sleep.

The next morning I was confronted by my doll... sat staring at me with a knife. I thought, *is this the end?* I was dead.

I come to warn people, *don't play with dolls!*

Zoe Loveridge (12)

King Alfred School, Highbridge

Forced

"I need to stop," I whisper to myself... I strain every muscle in my beaten body but his power is overwhelming. She's screaming and vigorously wriggling but the icy tendrils keep her firmly secured. I glance to my left and see him, the devilish man that's been terrorising me my whole life. His small, beady eyes go ghostly white and I can tell he's using all his evil power to control me.

The bloody knife in my hand creeps closer and closer to her horrified face as I hear a wicked, daunting laugh from the dark and haunting shadows.

Max Adams (12)

King Alfred School, Highbridge

The Girl In The Garden

"I need to stop," I whispered to myself. I stopped running. As I sat down under a tree, I couldn't hear my mum screaming anymore. I heard a *crack!* I froze. "H-h-hello?"
There was only silence as I calmed myself down. Then I heard a little girl. I stood up and ran. I stopped at an abandoned hospital. I heard another *crack* and suddenly, I was pushed in! *Thud!* As I looked up, I saw a black-haired girl in a hospital gown. I reached for my knife but it was too late. She raised her axe... then she laughed.

Emma Lloyd (12)
King Alfred School, Highbridge

The Figure

"Who was that?" Kobi asked.

June laughed, "It was a patient."

I turned around and told June to pack it in. We carried on down the hall and came across a room with patient files. June wanted to go through them.

Out of the corner of my eye, I saw a figure. I screamed.

They both asked me why I'd screamed, but my voice was frozen with fear. They looked around the room, trying to find what scared me, but they couldn't see it. Only me.

My hairs stood on end like static. Then I disappeared and all was black.

Rhiannon French (13)
King Alfred School, Highbridge

The Girl From My Nightmare Came To Life

I woke up at midnight from my nightmare because I heard a scream that echoed outside from the misty dark alley. When I was breathing heavily, another scream echoed outside. It was coming from the same misty, dark alley. A cold shiver dripped down my back. *Instead of controlling my own actions, my legs are controlling where I'm going,* I thought to myself. *Where am I going? Why am I going outside?*
As I was starting to get frightened, a girl was coming for me, but behind her, I saw a person lying on the floor, *dead.*

Poppy Holding (12)
King Alfred School, Highbridge

Big Bad Bully

"You have one chance, choose wisely," that's what I said to myself as I took my final breath. As I crawled to the fence, I read the sign: 'Keep out. Danger!' and I heard a voice whisper, "I knew you wouldn't listen, now this is your punishment."

I thought to myself, *what did I ever do to deserve this?* Then I remembered Suzy Parker. When I bullied her, she left home and was never seen again.

Suddenly, my knees went weak. All of a sudden, I felt a pair of hands grabbing me. What was going to happen?

Charlie Harper (12)
King Alfred School, Highbridge

The Expedition

"I need to stop," I whispered to myself and wondered who the next victim was.

After six hours of research, "I have finally found my next target, his name is Thomas Jacana. He owns a bank in northern Jamaica, I will execute him and take his money."

"Status report?"

"I'm en route to the bank and I'm going to sneak in the back when a colleague leaves it open."

I found the owner and interrogated him, got him to open the vault and killed him. I took his money but got caught by the police.

Kian Tett (12)
King Alfred School, Highbridge

The Bully That Killed

Today, Betty came over to me and was saying stuff to me. It sounded rude but I was too busy thinking of all the horrible things in my life. The only thing I remembered was, "Meet me in the graveyard, North East."

I had this feeling in my tummy, like my soul was draining out of me.

When I finally arrived at the foggy destination, the mist cleared. My name was on a moss-covered gravestone. Was I dead? Did I even exist? "I need to stop," I whispered to myself.

I heard the crunching of leaves behind me... *bang!*

Freyja-Jayne Hewlett (12)
King Alfred School, Highbridge

The End... But Of What?

I stand there, frozen solid in awe. I scramble some courage, enough to take two steps forward and wipe the repulsive moss off of my gravestone. It says that I die in three minutes... I can't control myself. I am breathing erratically as I sprint as fast as I can, ducking and dodging branches until I stumble over a log that's sticking out of the coarse earth. However it isn't a log...

I shriek and wail as loud as a wolf howling in the midnight moonlight. I scream for someone, anyone to help me... Suddenly, there's silence...

Grace Simmonds (13)

King Alfred School, Highbridge

Roller Coaster

Getting ready to go on the biggest roller coaster in the world, standing with my papa, getting into the one person seat, realising that I won't be with my only friend; knowing if I die, I won't be near my papa. Going up, my back right against the chair, not knowing what's going to be in the tunnel, lights, loops, twists and turns, now out of the tunnel. Now I'm going up the biggest roller coaster in the world, up we go, turning, ready to go down... *Boom!*
Then I slide off, going through the air... going to die...

Max Jack Samuels (13)
King Alfred School, Highbridge

Choose Or Die

I had to pick a side. A town split. Each with their pros and cons. The east was hectic with threatening gangs, dark scenery and creepy graveyards, but the most important thing; my family.

The west was luminous, charitable, but filled with shaken people thinking the east would attack. The terror of war emerged between them, making the sides more paranoid than welcoming. However, both were accepting me.

I knew I had to pick. I knew I couldn't be on both. I knew they could make it, so I was on neither side.

They would kill me...

Katie House (13)

King Alfred School, Highbridge

Cutting

I can't help it, it's like something is overtaking me, making me do stuff, forcing me. As I bring the knife up to my wrist, I'm trying to stop myself. I'm moving but for some reason my body won't listen to my mind! It's a truly horrible feeling, I feel like I am in a nightmare! I can't stop myself from doing anything. I feel like a voodoo doll! Like someone is controlling me!

As I cut my wrist, for some reason, I can't feel it! So without feeling, I keep on cutting and cutting until there's nothing left!

Ellen Sheerman (13)
King Alfred School, Highbridge

I See You

"You have one choice, choose wisely," those words of my father. "So, since you're grounded, the rest of the family and I decided to get a Chinese at the takeaway, so we felt kind enough to give you a choice. Go with us and *be kind and helpful,* or *stay home alone...?*"

"Easy, home alone! I'd rather be here than with you guys..." I bravely said.

So, I went to bed.

A set of eyes looked at me through my window. I was petrified!

Who and *what* was that thing?

Dan Hinks (12)

King Alfred School, Highbridge

One Chance

"You have one chance, choose wisely, truth or dare?" said Craig.

The boy answered, "Dare."

"Okay," said Craig, "throw this rubber at the teacher."

So he did. The rubber hit the teacher right on the head. The teacher turned around with fury in her eyes and turned into a demonic beast, gobbling the child up with one bite. Then she said, "If anyone thinks they can do that, then you must be mistaken. Now you can see what happened when you disobey the teacher! Now get on with your work."

Morgan Anderson-Kaye (13)
King Alfred School, Highbridge

Killing Fields

A blood-curdling scream echoed outside. I shouted back.
There was no answer. I looked out to the dark fields in front
of me. I shouted again. There was a ghastly sludgy noise,
like someone rummaging through someone's guts. I felt sick
but still, I ran to the noise. It was a humongous pig eating a
cabbage.
Suddenly, the pig dropped and died.
I looked behind me to see a long, bony man wearing a black
suit, walking towards me. His hands were bone, no flesh at
all.
Horrified, I realised it was my father. Then he turned to ash.

Thomas Harvey (12)
King Alfred School, Highbridge

There He Was!

Who on Earth was that? I thought to myself, as I woke up with a pale face, sweat dripped down my forehead with nervousness. My heart pumped as quickly as an F1 driver's. I unhurriedly tiptoed to my window to investigate who had screamed so miraculously.

I tiptoed down the creaky, squeaky, ancient (which didn't help) stairs, to the front door. As my hand shook like the San Francisco tectonic plates, there he was. My mouth opened in shock. My tremendous, fantastic life was over. I knew it was over. He had killed me.

Leo James (13)
King Alfred School, Highbridge

He

A scream echoed outside, so loud yet so distant. The scream echoed again, I fell. I got up and shakily crept to my window. I looked out, so dark but lots could be seen. When I looked behind me, there were red eyes.

Feeling intimidated, I stumbled to my wardrobe. I looked back, darkness overwhelmed my eyes, fear struck my heart, consuming it whole. My bed, which once was a block of wood with damp sheets, was now a bloody mattress.

I slammed the door in fear, he was here.

"I want to play with you, come out," he said.

Erin Dawson (11)
King Alfred School, Highbridge

The Chase

A scream echoed outside, followed by another deafening scream... They seemed to get louder and louder. It was pitch-black. The thunder clouds covered most of the sky. It started to shower with rain. I was down on my knees. I couldn't go any further. I had purple wounds on my legs and arms. I heard their footsteps getting closer. I had to move. I was cornered.

I stood up and saw their orange, glaring eyes. They came closer. They started to tear me apart. I could not feel my legs. They split me apart. This was the zombie apocalypse.

Mason Mcphee (12)
King Alfred School, Highbridge

Remember Me

I was stood up, just staring at the dead, white moon. I felt a deep, cold rush go through my body. I knew it was behind me, ready to push me into my deadly grave. It was mute, unapproachable, threatening and completely untouchable. I could feel his ice-cold devil breath breathing down the back of my spine. *Boom!* He threw my body into a smashed chestnut tree. My spine shattered. It looked down at me. It had crimson, bloodshot eyes, looking down at me. Was this the end of me? I took my last heartbeat. Goodbye world. It ended.

Juliette Clare Newing (13)
King Alfred School, Highbridge

Screams And Echoes

I hear a scream and echoes coming from the house. The fog comes in closer and closer to the graveyard. I go closer to the door of the petrifying house. I can still hear the screams coming from the house.

As I go up the creaking steps, there are eerie sounds coming across the graveyard.

Suddenly, the door opens slowly. I'm petrified. I head to the door, expecting something, or someone to be there.

I put my hand on the door handle and slowly open the door. All of a sudden, there's a dark figure staring at me...

Sophie Groom (12)
King Alfred School, Highbridge

The Hiding

A scream echoed outside of the asylum, it sounded like a girl, about fifteen years old... *wait!* That wasn't a random girl, it was my daughter!

Four hours ago... I woke up at 3am to find my daughter not there! Wait, she'd left a note saying she'd been kidnapped. I needed to find her!

Deep into the mist, I found the location of my daughter, an asylum in downtown London. I could hear her screams.

I found the room where she was. I ran and *bang!* I'd been shot. Was my daughter okay? Was I okay?

Harvey Fisher (12)
King Alfred School, Highbridge

The Midnight Clear

I remembered his last words, "This is the beginning of the end..." I couldn't get over it, my best friend, dead in front of me because of the mistake I made, taking her to the most haunted area in The Dead Forest. Of course, that wasn't its real name, the real name was Anagonkia, which translated to never-ending forest. I found the area that was most haunted, I took her there. I dared her to go in the cave nicknamed *the cave of terrible deaths*. I heard a scream but it was too late, I should have trusted her...

Michael John Oliver (13)
King Alfred School, Highbridge

The Cookie Quest

A scream echoed outside. I thought this was my chance. I tiptoed down the fluffy but stiff stairs, I heard a creak in the wooden floor. I swiftly and rapidly snuck to the kitchen and carefully climbed up the handles of the drawers and silently opened the cupboard. There it was. I thought it was beautiful. The cookie jar!

I gently snatched it and carefully climbed down. Back I went across the squeaky floor and up the stiff and fluffy stairs. *Here I go*, I thought, but then I heard the dreadful sound of the door. It was Mom!

Artur Vasile (11)

King Alfred School, Highbridge

Following...

A scream echoes outside... I sit silently, not moving a muscle until I know the coast is clear.

I walk slowly outside and I hear it again. I keep walking until I reach the end of the road. Then I hear counting... five... four... three... two... I run until my legs can't keep me up. I collapse on a bench. I hear the screaming again, it's getting closer!

I try to stand up but my legs can't hold me. The counting starts again, but this time I sit and don't move. Somebody is screaming but I know it isn't me...

Rebecca Hall (12)

King Alfred School, Highbridge

You Have One Chance

"You have one chance, choose wisely..."
Grandad always said these words to me, all because when I was little, my mama and papa died. I was only three. My grandad now wanted me to make the most of my life and do everything three times better for them.
My grandad had brought me up since I was three. I couldn't ever remember Mama and Papa. My first memory was on my fourth birthday and Grandad gave me a bike.
Now I was thirteen and I missed Mama and Papa even more. I would never forget how much I loved them.

Jasmine Haines (13)
King Alfred School, Highbridge

Zone 66

I remembered his last words, "This is the beginning of the end." Now, I thought, I was starting to believe him. In my world, there were zones, like big stone mazes, full of your worst nightmares. Which led me to the day it all ended. My friend and I were playing baseball when the floor opened up; a big, red button appeared. I told him not to touch it, but he did. A loud, clunking sound erupted. It was so loud we couldn't hear anything but the dreadful noise. Then the doors opened to all the zones. We were doomed!

Jessica Longley (12)
King Alfred School, Highbridge

Mystery

They said I was a traitor but I wasn't.

We came to this house for a reunion but now we were stuck with someone. We heard creaking upstairs when no one was there.

Everyone split up and I was scared. My friend went to check out a room. It'd been five minutes since he'd gone in and I'd just been hiding behind a door.

I heard something coming down the hall. I held my breath for as long as I could, but then it started running. Someone was chasing it.

I ran to the door and it creaked open, freedom!

Oliver Jones-Hawkins (11)

King Alfred School, Highbridge

Electric Life

I was shocked, in awe. My life was a lie. I... was artificial.

I looked at my wires. I didn't know what to think. If I was artificial, then what was everyone else? Human, or android? Everything... was a lie.

I ripped my skin coating off of my arm, exposing a robotic arm. I ripped off my face in a fit of rage, not seeing flesh, but a head of pure machine, protecting a memory card. I decided... everything was a lie, so I destroyed my memory card.

If everything I lived for was true, then I could live thankfully.

James Hewlett (13)
King Alfred School, Highbridge

Late In The Fog

I was shocked. It definitely came from a far distance.
I ran outside to check but it was foggy and I couldn't see anything from where I stood. I walked closer, into the fog. I was freezing cold but didn't want to go back. I kept walking forwards and out of nowhere, there was a black, tall figure, stood still, facing me.
I kept as quiet as I could in case I hadn't been noticed yet, so I went back home and switched all the lights out and stayed quiet. But I heard a scream again...
I ran back downstairs.

Ellie-Grace Newman (13)
King Alfred School, Highbridge

Electric Blood

Blood stood around me like a cave of rubies reflecting the face of an assassin. *This* was what I had been built to do? I felt a sharp, mechanical hand on my shoulder. I twisted my head around to the impulsive machine. I reached to detach my arm to grab my gun. *Bang!* I shot it clean and dead. I put my arm back in my socket to see lights stabbing through the sky. I turned around to see the 'dead' machine with a mallet in its lethal hands. I gazed in disbelief. Was this the end or the beginning?

India Porter (13)
King Alfred School, Highbridge

The Grave Rave

My death was dated today!

Running towards the exit, I saw my mother's grave not so far from my own. As I knelt down, the ground started to shake. A skeleton hand appeared from her grave. "Mum?" I squealed.

She climbed out of the grave, in one hand was a shovel. She started creeping towards me. I thought it would be best to back away. She kept advancing.

This was when I tripped, my grave was there. I fell into my grave and my mum started filling it with mud.

This was the end for me, or was it?

Rhys Anderson (12)
King Alfred School, Highbridge

Victim 7: Paris

"I need to stop," I whispered to myself as I looked at my blood-covered hands, "this is serious."
I looked at the body by my feet. Her neck was twisted in an unusual position and there was a golf club sticking out of her stomach. Blood pooled all around my feet as I looked at her dead body. I didn't like what I was doing, but in some way, it was satisfying to see the life leave her eyes.
I pushed her body into the hole and buried her with dirt and leaves.
"Jennie, is that you?"

Lily Evans (12)
King Alfred School, Highbridge

They Say I'm A Traitor

They said I was a traitor...

... for helping him escape. What I did was what I thought was right. I needed information about my parents; who they were, if they were alive. I was going to meet them tonight, under the bridge.

I was here, but where were they? I could hear something from the bushes. Was it them? It was not. It was a wolf, it was coming for me.

There was now more of them surrounding me. *What do I do?* I was doomed.

Wait.

There was a trapdoor. I was going in! *Please God let there be something good there...*

William Gardner (12)
King Alfred School, Highbridge

Pure Evil Returns!

The mist cleared, my name was on the moss-covered grave. I thought, *it's a mistake.* I clawed at the moss to reveal a name, but it still said 'James Lancaster'. The death date said it was today. I saw a claw mark on top!

Suddenly, I heard a bush rattle and a stick crack. I turned my flashlight to the bush and felt a hand on my shoulder. I quickly turned, it was Jane, my mother. She said we had to go now.

As we were leaving, I saw a devilish pair of luminous red eyes staring with great intent...

Malachi Crozier (12)
King Alfred School, Highbridge

Beginning Of The End...

I remembered his last words: "This is the beginning of the end..."

Now, let me recap what happened before the life drained out of my father.

A day before that, I was a normal teenage girl who was grumpy but living my life on the edge. We were a healthy family, but the next day, we were having a discussion, my father and I, about life and what I was doing at school (I was pretty reckless). But the unexpected happened... his heart turned as cold as ice and his face like a sheet of paper. He was dead...

Amy Skinner (11)
King Alfred School, Highbridge

The Knife

"I need to stop," I whispered to myself, but it made no difference. I wasn't listening. I felt like I was being controlled, my hand was sliding along the pristine counter in the kitchen, no control over it. As silent as the wind, I crept along to the knife drawer. Feeling but not thinking, moving but not controlling.

I reached for the knife, snatching it out of the drawer. Silently I slid back up the stairs when I realised what I was doing. Frantically, I tried to regain control of my body but failed.

Kevina Williams (11)
King Alfred School, Highbridge

Guardian Angel

A cold night on the railway station, 1953, I decided to sit in the waiting room. I thought I was alone but in the corner was a kind old lady. "Hello," I said.

She looked up and smiled at me.

About ten minutes had passed, then the station master came in. He asked me if I would like a cup of tea. I said, "No thank you, maybe that lady would like one?"

He looked at me and screamed as he ran out. The lady was a ghost that saved me from dangers. Our guardian angels come in different forms.

Teigan Bateman (11)
King Alfred School, Highbridge

My Mini Saga

I remembered his last words: "This is the beginning of the end." What did he mean? I was confused for days and days, but I quickly flashed back to the day before he died.
This was it, the war had begun. The Killer Dark Coal had a strong army, way stronger than the both of us. Captain Agent Stark Collins was a funny joker and a brilliant mind, with amazing strength and athletic abilities. Sadly, he lived a depressing life, his parents ran away when he was two, and then he was stabbed, on that fateful day.

Leon Llewellyn (12)
King Alfred School, Highbridge

The Upside-Down World

"Ouch!" Instead of blood there were wires. I'd fallen on a piece of rusty, corrugated metal. Pain shot down my arm as fine wires grew from my pale skin. Suddenly, my surroundings swirled and I fell.

As soon as I opened my eyes I could see my family around me. "Mum?"

"Hello, Ana." As she spoke, thick blood dripped out of her mouth. My brother, sister, mum and dad were all covered in wires. It was then I remembered the crash through the fence and towards the abandoned cottage.

Polly Tottle (12)

King Alfred School, Highbridge

The Day I Will Never Forget

A scream echoed outside. It was coming from the field. The dark, abandoned, field.

My heart was beating rapidly in my chest as I sprinted to go help them, but it was too late. I couldn't save them, it was the new neighbours; a little girl and her dad.

I remembered his last words: "This is the beginning, and the end." It was the worst day of my life. It was a day I would never forget. From that day on, it was never the same. Every time I heard someone scream, I thought back to that day...

Bethan Sinclair (12)
King Alfred School, Highbridge

What Have I Done?

A scream echoed outside, it sent a shiver down my spine. I heard sirens, louder than ever. What had I gotten myself into? I ran into a nearby house and ran my blood-covered hands down the damp walls. Then I heard him again, no one else could hear him but I knew he was real. All I heard him say was, "Kill."

My eyes started burning with rage. I clenched the knife from my belt. I looked around the corner to see my daughter; I could not disobey Master's orders.

Next thing I knew, she lay, dead...

Ruby Amber-Mae Clements (12)
King Alfred School, Highbridge

The Chameleon Who Stole Bubblegum

Today was a different day, the chameleon found that he loved gum. He blew gum 24/7 without stopping. Soon, he came to his last piece. He blew his last bubble. It popped and coloured him pink!

He ran to the shops and stole some because he found he was well disguised. He ran through the shelves, knocking things off. He was losing his colour!

The chameleon fell off a shelf and when he had landed, the shopkeeper ran over to help. The chameleon was in shock, but he still ran over and took a pile of bubblegum!

Vibeke Lovise Farnsworth (12)
King Alfred School, Highbridge

The Fall

It was dark, I couldn't see where I was going. Suddenly, I heard a scream. It echoed through the woods. It sounded like Bella.

I ran and ran until all I could see was pitch-black. I walked a little further and suddenly I fell. It felt like I was falling forever. I stopped with a thud. I could see something. It was bright. Then I could see a figure. It was Bella.

I hobbled to her. She was injured but she was alright. She asked me why I was hobbling. I said I thought I'd twisted something, badly...

Neve Lacey (11)
King Alfred School, Highbridge

A Strange Thing

A deathly scream came from outside of my bedroom window. "Should I look out?" I said to myself. The hairs on the back of my neck started to stick up and I could not go back to sleep. What should I do? I looked out of my window and to my despair, I saw a sack wriggling on the pavement out on the street. *What could it be?* I wondered.

I started to walk to my door, thinking about what was in the sack. I walked downstairs. "Should I go outside?" I kept saying to myself. I went outside!

Joseph Street (11)
King Alfred School, Highbridge

The Mysterious Creature

A scream echoed outside. I ran outside to see a human-like body on the ground. I went towards it.

As I got closer, I heard a droning noise. The body disappeared but I could feel someone breathing down my neck. I turned around to see a hideous creature; in its eyes you could see death itself.

I ran as fast as I could, the creature running close behind me. I ran towards the woods and carried on running until I realised it was a dead end.

The creature had trapped me in a corner. I knew I was dead now.

Andreas Laoutaris (11)
King Alfred School, Highbridge

The Scream

I wondered what it was, I went outside into the black night. I got pulled back to the wall. He had a mask so I couldn't see who it was. He said in a strange voice, "You are lucky." In a second, he vanished.

That night, I couldn't go to bed, thinking about him staring at me.

The next day, I saw strange things, like shadows. I knew that he was following me. I could feel a breeze rushing past me. He took me and pulled me along. He took a knife out and stabbed it through my stomach. Blood!

Madison James (13)
King Alfred School, Highbridge

Tapping

"You have one chance, choose wisely," my mother said as she and my family were leaving for a night out. "You've been grounded, you either stay home *alone*, or come with us and *behave*."

I wanted to be like the cool kids in my school so I stayed home. I thought I'd go to sleep, but all of a sudden, I heard a mysterious noise from the window. I peered behind me and looked out the window, before my eyes there was a shadow cast in my room.

Then, I made a decision.

Jacob Porter (12)
King Alfred School, Highbridge

Only One Chance

On the night of the disappearance, there was a group of friends partying in the old, abandoned mansion. Little did they know that the mansion wasn't abandoned. There were people 'living' in the basement, but they weren't exactly living.
It was too late to leave, they had their chance. Had they taken it, they might have made it home that night to speak to their family one last time. But it was too late and so they were taken, not to teach others a lesson, but to make sure they never came back.

Thomas Walter (13)
King Alfred School, Highbridge

I Remembered

The mist cleared and my name was on the moss-covered gravestone. I sat there, staring. I had one question: *how did I die?* For some reason, I did not want to leave.

I lay down and that was when I remembered what happened.

It was Christmas Eve, 1801, I was walking and a man ran past me. He gave me an object.

The next thing I knew, I was buried alive with a bomb on my heart.

Today was Halloween 2018, and I was in front of my gravestone. Who was I?

I guess you might never find out!

Poppy Kilduff (11)
King Alfred School, Highbridge

Help

The mist clears and my name's on the moss-covered gravestone, so of course, I run. I don't know where though. I don't have a clue, but I still run. Oh no, I trip. "Argh!" A horrible, purple beast surges out of the shadows and tries to grab me. I swerve. Oh no, I'm at a dead end. Oh no, the beast squelches towards me! "Help!" I punch out and my fist goes through his body. Oh God, his jaws are so enormous. I try to pull my arm out and fall back into a dungeon. "Argh!"

Aleisha Baker (12)
King Alfred School, Highbridge

Compelled

I didn't know what to choose. I either rip his heart out of his cold, bloodless body, or be tortured for the rest of my life. I had to choose, so I chose to rip his heart out.
I walked to his dark house, filled with secrets. I rang his doorbell. It made a loud screech as he slowly opened the door. Cold air whooshed out into my face, making me stone-cold. I walked towards him, my hands at the ready. I put my hand on his chest, then ripped his heart out. Blood everywhere.
I fell. What happened...?

Niamh Madeline Criddle (13)
King Alfred School, Highbridge

Him

The screams sound fuzzy. I open my eyes to see I'm in a dark room of some kind. I try to stand but I get tugged back down. The shackles cut through my skin, allowing blood to spill out. "How did I get here?" is all I can ask myself. I try and move my legs but it burns and I hear my bones snap. Tears roll down my cheeks. I pull harder on my shackles, tearing my skin more, the hot, red fluid leaks out of my cold wrists. The door creaks open, revealing a human's silhouette.

It's him...

Scarlett Morris (12)
King Alfred School, Highbridge

The House

Screams ran inside as I stood outside of the door. They said there was no one there, I wondered what they'd hidden from me.

Getting closer, their screams came more loudly until... *crash!* Something fell but no one was in the house.

I carefully placed my sweaty palms, the frozen door handle gave me chills down my spine. I was being watched (and I was correct).

I felt something go down my spine but turned to see nothing but my loneliness.

"Hello, who's there...?"

Samantha Fisher (12)

King Alfred School, Highbridge

The Maze Of Death

A scream echoed from around the corner. I came to a halt, then heard it again but this time much louder, it sounded like it was coming towards me.

Suddenly, the steps and screaming stopped. In front of me, I saw blood oozing out of a corner and a strong, black shadow projected onto the wall.

It was midnight, I was in the maze of death. I didn't know why, didn't know how, all I knew was I fell asleep and woke up. So all I could do was run and that was when it started. I heard the scream...

Jack Richardson (11)
King Alfred School, Highbridge

Help Me Now

I asked what was happening and then ran out. All of a sudden, I saw my dad who'd passed away a year ago, sprinting towards me. He dragged me down to the ground. I desperately gasped for air. What should I do now?
"Someone help!"
I woke up, he was there, looking down into my soul. Then, all of a sudden, I saw bruises come up like snakes crawling up my legs. I knew something was wrong.
The laugh of death reached my ears. Now I knew what he had done.
"Someone help me!"

Rosetta Luxon (12)
King Alfred School, Highbridge

Death's Lair

I started wondering what was going on and what I was. The land was covered in mist with some patches of red. The wires led me to a patch. I knelt down and saw a person covered in blood, no eyes, empty.

I looked further down the body and there were no legs, just guts. It was cut with precision by a massive blade.

"Ow!" more wires came out but this time they led to a shadowy figure with eyes made of blood. The reaper and his merciless, monstrous and deformed pet looked directly at me...

Kamil Gabriel Majdczak (13)

King Alfred School, Highbridge

Crash

We hit the floor with a crash. We were lost. Jack hit a gravestone, it said, 'We are coming for you.'
Peter went into a hole full of bones. Jess fell into a tree. We tried to find each other. Eventually we bumped into each other.
We collected sticks, then made a fire, then went to bed.
In the roasting hot morning, we tried to find a way out. All of a sudden, a box of food dropped out of the sky and hit the floor. More and more donkeys fell out of the sky and jumped over the cave!

Morgan Fear (11)
King Alfred School, Highbridge

My Mini Saga

The mist cleared and my name was on the moss-covered gravestone. It was a sad day for my family, people were crying, but one person was happy I was dead, it was my dad.

"Hey Dad, can the family go to the park?"

"Yes."

That was a bad mistake.

"Hey son, come here, I think there's gold in this bush."

"Okay!" So I went and he put a knife in my arm. I quickly got the knife and I fell over and was dying while my dad showed his true self.

Bradley Waite (11)
King Alfred School, Highbridge

Sadness

"You have one chance, choose wisely..." I was about to sell my soul to the Devil to save him, to save his innocent and pure heart. I needed him, I would always need him.

It was a winter's night and my brother was outside playing in the snow when he collapsed. He had been in a coma for years and I was going to do anything to watch him play in the snow one more time. There was only one way I could possibly help. To leave and let that monster help him.

It chilled me to the bone.

Lauren Summer Lewis (13)
King Alfred School, Highbridge

Bed Of Horror

A scream echoed outside for help... "What was that?" I said to myself. All there was was a fence in front of me and I had to get away, but I did not see the fence sign saying: 'Beware the house'.

I jumped onto the fence and over. I cut myself, blood all over me. I ran into the house, limping and upstairs into a bedroom to slam the door, and that was my mistake. I saw a dark, thin shadow in the bed and wondered what it was, and whatever it was leapt out at me. "Argh!"

Liam Burrow (12)
King Alfred School, Highbridge

The Mystical Creature

In the dark night, I didn't know if I should've looked outside or not, but I did and what I saw would never leave my mind. It wasn't pleasant, it wasn't kind. I had to quickly close my blinds.

What I saw was a man, or should I say a creature, and that creature had looked straight into my eyes. Lying next to it was a woman covered in blood. I was scared. I hid under my bed. The floors started to creak. I started to shiver. The creaks got louder and louder, but it was just my cat.

Elliot Harris (13)
King Alfred School, Highbridge

Man In The Mist

I looked at three victims and realised what I had done. I had a bitter taste in my mouth. I looked into the distance. I swung around to see nothing but thick mist.

I saw a figure darting in the mist. I dared not speak. I couldn't believe what I'd done. I felt like a monster. Maybe I was a monster.

I saw iron gates around me. How was I going to escape this nightmare? I was trapped. What was I going to do?

I started to run but suddenly I felt hands on my shoulders. Who was it?

Millie Jones (12)

King Alfred School, Highbridge

The Blue Man

I was in my house, waiting for my mum to get home from hairdressing. She was one hour late. I hadn't seen anyone for about that time so I went outside and saw a frozen person, so I went to investigate.

Three objects moving fast flew over my head. I ran back inside but then I heard sounds in my attic, so I hid under my bed.

All I could hear were footsteps over and over again. I ran for the door, then I saw a blue man running and running. Before I could say something, I was frozen too.

Joseph Fitzpatrick (11)
King Alfred School, Highbridge

Puppies

It was a Wednesday night. I was at my nan's and having tea. We had pasta. My nan had a dog called Poppy. We always called her Pop though.

Poppy was having puppies soon. I had a sleepover at my nan's. It was around six o'clock in the morning. A scream echoed inside. I ran as fast as I could and puppies were on her bed.

I ran as fast as I could to wake up my nan. We went and got my phone, took pictures and washed them.

When it was around seven thirty, we got to hold them.

Amy Denvir (11)
King Alfred School, Highbridge

Spare The Shot

We'd agreed on three meeting places. I'd just reached the last one...

... Then I saw *him*, stood on a stool with a rope around his neck. He told me to run but then, out they came, the neighbourhood gang. They tormented me with thousands and thousands of pounds but I couldn't leave him. I told them no. Then they shut the door and grabbed me and held me. I was about to get shot, but then I asked them, "What did he do?"
The man lifted the gun and shot the ground, he told me and James to run off. We'd never told the story to anyone, ever.

Zak Lewis (12)
King Alfred School, Highbridge

My Mini Saga

The mist cleared and my name was on the moss-covered gravestone with my mum standing next to it, crying. Then I heard a bang. It was just a dream.

The following day, my mates and I went to the park. When we got there, I saw something unusual. It was an electric fence, it said: 'Danger! Keep out!'

Being curious, I decided to see what was in there. My friends told me to get away but I just ignored them. There was a little hole in the fence just big enough for me to fit through...

Leo Durrant (11)
King Alfred School, Highbridge

Bad Candy

"I need to stop," I whispered to myself. My head was telling me to go back, but my gut told me to go. I climbed over the fence, nearly cutting my arm as I jumped down on the other side. I ran to the double doors, bursting them open. There was a loud *bang!*

As I turned a corner, I nearly fell into a giant, boiling chocolate river. As I stepped back, I fell down a hole which brought me to a big table filled with popping candy. I tried some and then I saw the end of my life!

Sophie Chislett (12)
King Alfred School, Highbridge

Make A Difference In Time...

"You have one chance, choose wisely," I heard a whisper in my ear as the skies turned grey. There, before me, was a choice, the part of my life when my opinion mattered to the world. The voice echoed in my mind, telling me that I had to set things straight.

There were two buttons, one for 100 years in the past, and one for 100 years in the future. I had one chance.

In the past, I had the power to end World Wars, in the future I'd be stuck in a nuclear bomb attack...

Tegan Louise Kelleher (11)

King Alfred School, Highbridge

Five Plagues Of Egypt

I remembered his last words: "This is the beginning of the end."

The temple of the Egyptian gods. When I entered, the feeling of power surged in me. There was a golden statue of all the gods and I was going to be the first to see them. I saw where my father had failed but I would succeed. I could see the glimmer of gold around the sturdy pillars. The room was full of gold and it was all mine. But the gold was cursed and I didn't know the five plagues of Egypt had begun.

Alessandro Salamanca (11)
King Alfred School, Highbridge

Forgotten

I didn't know how, I didn't know when, but I was dead. It was for sure. I felt the leftover, ghostly parts of me drop. I floated back into the distance and was forgotten. I didn't know what to say or do. All I knew is that it was over. I was bored, I was angry, sat there for years and years! Doing nothing. I had no one, nor anything, except my broken soul. I wanted to be alive, I wanted to be with family, but I was dead. I wanted to have friends and have fun. I was dead.

Callum Sinnett Priestley (13)
King Alfred School, Highbridge

My Mini Saga Story

A scream echoed outside. We walked into the base with five troops, on a mission to find the leader of Satan with a base the size of forty houses together.

We saw Satan, my sniper was about to get him until he saw us and his men rushed down to kill us but I had a minigun and they were torn apart.

His men were strong but my men and I were stronger than all of them together. We broke out of there in time to get back to our own base. Then the enemies were killed, or were they?

Kyle Higgs (12)
King Alfred School, Highbridge

Time To Come Home

The mist clears and my name's on the moss-covered gravestone. What is this? How did this happen? I'm full of questions.

Then I hear my ringtone echoing in the wind. I answer. "It's time to come home Jack."

I put my phone away. I can feel the cold biting at my legs. However it isn't the cold, it's the cold, white, ghastly hand of a skeleton. It says, "It's time to come home Jack."

I can feel my life force slipping away...

Christian William Whyte (12)
King Alfred School, Highbridge

A Success Or An Explosion

At a construction site, the workers found a familiar object, *a bomb*.

They found a timer and a box that said the bomb was going to explode the Earth if the timer ran out of time. The workers panicked as they had about a minute left. A worker came to the front and spoke. "Lads, we only have a few seconds left until we find ourselves in grave danger, however we can cut one rope with my scissors."

The worker cut one of the ropes... *Baaaannngggg!*

Harley Buncombe (11)

King Alfred School, Highbridge

Mini Saga Story

"I need to stop," I whispered to myself. I heard an echo but it wasn't my voice. It was pitch-black, I didn't know where to go. A light flickered in the distance, I followed it and suddenly I was in a car full of blood.

The car started to move, I was the only person in it. I heard a voice in the boot. I didn't know what to do.

Suddenly, the car stopped and a man got out of the boot, he grabbed me and threw me out. But I thought I was dreaming.

Louis Clarke (12)
King Alfred School, Highbridge

The Mist

I needed to get away from the mist, it was affecting me. There was a stabbing feeling in my brain. I began to hear a voice in my head, "Come closer, I can help." It kept calling to me, I had this urge to drag my body towards it. I couldn't resist, but I knew I had to.

The thought of what could be beyond the mist was irresistible. I had to get out, the fog was so thick, it was like my eyes had been sucked out of me.

I turned to go, but then it got me.

Sienna Field (13)
King Alfred School, Highbridge

A Psychopathic Murderer

A scream echoed outside. My parents had always told me to stay away from the misty woods, but just last night I was told why; it was because a psychopathic murderer that had been exiled from our village had made it his home. Every week he would sneak into the village under the cover of darkness and steal a child to murder.

All of us had been taught what to do if he chose us: bite, kick and scream for our father who would sprint in with a rifle or shotgun to shoot him.

Rory Kerton (12)
King Alfred School, Highbridge

Day 21 Of The Zombie Invasion

I remember his last words as if it were yesterday, "Remember me." I needed to stop dwelling on the fact that my little brother was dead, he died a slow and painful death. He was eaten alive by man-eating zombies, along with many others, including my mother and father. I could still hear their screams for help. I only wished I had gotten to them quicker. Now it was just me all alone against a zombie apocalypse. I didn't know if there were any more survivors...

Oakley Jai Timms (12)
King Alfred School, Highbridge

The Lab Of Death

A scream echoes outside. I wake up and I look outside and there is a person out there and he's holding a gun to me. I scream and hide. I hear a door creak open and I fall asleep and I wake up in a lab with a scaly, green, mutated monster next to me.

I struggle but I can't escape. They let the monster out to run but then they let me out to run and hide. There's gas everywhere. I cough and hear a *creak, crack, snap.*

I have to hide or die...!

Korben Phillip Thomas Noble (11)

King Alfred School, Highbridge

The Asylum

A scream echoed outside the asylum. My brother and I ran as fast as we could to go get my sister, but when we were on the second floor, we saw a room door open! There was a girl in there, rocking back and forth in the corner. There was blood leaking from her mouth.

Suddenly, she bolted at us and it was at this moment we realised it was our sister! The girl chased us up to the third floor, and then she stopped, grabbed some keys, and started to let the others out...

Mackenzie Crook (12)
King Alfred School, Highbridge

Hell

"You've one chance, choose it wisely." This was the last thing I heard before everything went dark. My whole life flashed before my ungrateful eyes. There were six doors. They each said '666' on them. This was the biggest choice I'd ever made, if it went wrong I'd never see my close friends or the ones I loved again.

I picked the sixth door. I heard demonic laughing and someone said, "You're staying here forever..."

Freddie Hatchard (12)
King Alfred School, Highbridge

My Mini Saga

A scream echoes outside with a bellowing tone to it. It's been a couple of seconds and I can still hear the scream floating through the air like a plane about to crash, but wait, it stops.

I sprint out to see who it is, but there is nothing. Then suddenly the sky turns as black as coal and before I can figure it out, I have been sucked into the sky, never to be seen, *ever again*.

Archy Ferguson (12)

King Alfred School, Highbridge

Ice Cream

"You have one chance, choose wisely. Ice cream or lollipop?" I bought an ice cream. I heard my baby crying so I ran to the car. The weather was cheerful. My kids ran around in the park. I called my kids and got in the car and drove home. I went to the back garden, got a chair out and relaxed in the sun. I had a drink of wine and some chocolate.

Grace Reading (12)
King Alfred School, Highbridge

The Ragamuffins

"Ouch!" Instead of blood there were wires. "Oh, that hurts!"
"Don't chicken out."
My friend, older brother and I were very different. I was careful, he was daring.
"God, that dog nearly bit a lump off me."
"We're not leaving until we get a few chickens, we need the money!"
Looking at the gash on my arm, I noticed it had turned a sickly green. Then it hit me.
"The farmer poisoned the wire." Before I could say anything else, my legs gave way and everything went dark. The last things I heard were the muffled cries of my brother.

Archie Waymouth (14)
Kings Of Wessex Academy, Cheddar

Synth

Inspired by Fallout 4

"Ouch..." Instead of blood there were wires, he was a synth, generation two. Thankfully, he didn't have one of those horrifying mannequin faces like the previous version had. I carried on, shooting my way through these machines pretending to be people. Thankfully, their guns were useless, my T-45B armour made the bullets bounce right off, but I could still feel the endless thuds as they hit me. The hydraulic system built into my suit allowed me to push on, even though I was fatigued from three days of fighting. Eventually, I made it, I reached the institute.

David Warren King (14)
Kings Of Wessex Academy, Cheddar

Extreme Parenting

The scream echoed outside the window, from the girl who was standing next to her callous parents. The girl was frantically waving her grey-coloured hands above her head whilst her parents were trying to pin her down.

In my head, I was saying to myself, *I know these people. The girl is vivacious and versatile but her parents are callous people who are abhorrent to their daughter. They're excessively crazy.*

I came out of my daydream and that was when I heard what was being said to the girl who was pinned to the ground by her parents...

Lydia Menear (13)
Kings Of Wessex Academy, Cheddar

The Scream

A scream echoes outside. I step outside. Wind howls through the clouds; the sky as black as soot. The scream rings through my brain. Everything I know is forgotten, except the feeling of fear. Again, the same deathly scream. Reluctantly, I grip the door, my other hand quickly follows but a frightening urge stops me from going inside. Suddenly, the sickening scream reoccurs right next to me, right behind me, right inside my house.
Sweat drips rapidly off my head as I conjure up a plan... nothing. Clueless, I step inside my house...

Erin Hemms (14)
Kings Of Wessex Academy, Cheddar

Dead Money

"I need to stop," I whispered to myself, as the lock of the rusted gate fell to the floor. I shuddered as a cool breeze whipped around my bare feet and exposed chest. My ragged trench coat hung down to my knees. Fashion choice was hardly my best trait.

I braved the cold and started pacing my way to the moss-covered tombstone which lay under my gaze. "Just a little more money and then I'm never coming back." I fumbled around between the bones of the late Thomson Walker, looking for a necklace, a ring, anything...

Kell Gardner (14)
Kings Of Wessex Academy, Cheddar

Translucence

The mist cleared and my name was on the moss-covered gravestone. I reached out to touch the stone and trace the letters, my white hand went straight through.

Pinching myself, I thought I must be dreaming, therefore I tried again but it appeared like my sense of touch had vanished like a rabbit from a hat.

Suddenly, I looked around - I could see nothing. I could smell death and hear the wind whistling through the naked, rotting, dead trees. Slowly, my gaze turned to my hand - I could read my name through it.

I was a ghost.

Abigail Campbell (14)
Kings Of Wessex Academy, Cheddar

Pick Your Poison

"You have one chance, choose wisely," the witch doctor cackled after stating these words, tears of laughter falling onto the dying girl's face. The two bottles of murky liquid sat on the stand in front of me. One contained liquid cyanide, the other a healing elixir. I had to drink one, the dying girl, the other. Her life or mine.
The only catch, she had the power to save the world.
Surprise, surprise, I didn't.
I gingerly took one of the bottles into my hand.
"Bottoms up I guess..."

Sophie Angell (14)
Kings Of Wessex Academy, Cheddar

Power

I remembered his last words: "This is the beginning of the end..."
I didn't know what he meant at the time, but after he died, I got angry. It was ten years ago. I was only five when it happened. They took me away. I thought about it every day. I didn't remember much, just his last day. I thought he'd been in a fight?
After it happened, Mum and Dad left me. I was alone in a cold, dark room. I could control my powers now, maybe they would come back?
Was this what he'd meant?

Rachel Stockley (16)
Kings Of Wessex Academy, Cheddar

Creeping Tech

I remembered his last words: "This is the beginning of the end..." What did he mean by that? I didn't have the chance to ask any questions before he left. Panic rippled through me; I couldn't move. This was going to make looking for an escape a lot more difficult. I was surrounded by wires and cables, two bright lights gazed down at me. He was watching me.

I snapped my head around the room only to be faced with a series of computers, all showing the same thing... me.

Natasha Stewart (14)
Kings Of Wessex Academy, Cheddar

Robotic Extension

"Ouch..." Instead of blood there were wires. I was running and I cut myself on a tree branch. Why wasn't there blood? Why could I see wires?

The trees blew around violently and the whistling wind howled. I ran for my life until I came to a graveyard. I stopped. I turned to face a grave and saw my own name - 'Died 1937'.

All my life I'd thought I was a human. How was this possible? I couldn't believe this. Was I a robot? Argh! What would happen next?

Jemima Beatrice Ryles (13)
Kings Of Wessex Academy, Cheddar

The Way Back

The mist clears and my name's on the moss-covered gravestone. I'm standing, shocked, wondering, *what happened? How did I get here?*
A void appears behind me. "Haven't you figured it out yet?" they ask me.
"Figured out what? Am I dead?" I desperately shout.
"You aren't dead yet..." it says, "you're close."
"What do you mean?" I say, shivering with fear.
"You must find the way back," they whisper, "the way back to the corporeal world."
So this is the plane? Or an out-of-body experience? The confusion clears and I know what must be done.

Jack Crosweller (14)
St Dunstan's School, Glastonbury

Make A Choice

"You have one chance, choose wisely..." Those were the words that stayed with me. I was stumped. What choice did I need to make? It could be anything...

"Oi! How many times do I have to ask?" bellowed the dinner lady. "Peas or beans?"

"Uh, umm, oh, ooh... uh, p-p-pea-no, b-no..."

"Come on! You don't have to choose that carefully! Now, or I'll pick by myself!"

"Peas!" I sensed horror in the cold, damp air as she took a big scoop and dumped it onto my plate. And then I realised, I should have known; *I don't like those peas!*

James Manley (11)
St Dunstan's School, Glastonbury

Blooming Branches

"Ouch!" Instead of blood there were wires, they stuck out like branches. Within seconds, blooming fluorescent orange lights threw themselves onto the battered, lifeless platforms of the abandoned train station. The moon drew elusive, hard to picture, just like the pale fog, suffocating him with every short breath yet oblivious to the events surrounding him. His head turned in a nasty glance, his eyes rolled away and it began. All the fifteen years he had been directed in the way of never-ending disasters, punished for not being 'normal'. Now in captivity, he was trapped, forever and always.

Ruby Warwick Brown (13)
St Dunstan's School, Glastonbury

Intergalactic Arachnophobia

An alarm screamed across the ship. The ship shook. The crew manned their stations. Space pirates fired volleys of laser beams at the ship.

Meanwhile, inside the cruiser, Captain Lucifer leapt into an escape pod. He launched himself into the coldness of space. Flaming and smoking, the escape pod crashed into a planet. Lucifer's arachnophobia was about to be realised as he exited the escape hatch.

An automated voice exclaimed, "Have a nice day!" as he stepped onto the hill where he'd landed.

He could just make out in the distance, someone with eight arms waving at him...

Finlay Daniel Joseph Milton (12)

St Dunstan's School, Glastonbury

The Graveyard

The mist cleared and my name was on the moss-covered gravestone. Sticks snapped behind me. Owls whistled, bones clattered. The church bell struck twelve with a deafening high-pitched squeal. The church gates opened with a *creak*. I jumped out of my skin.
Trees cast shadows towering over me. I ran as fast as I could. It felt like someone was trailing behind me.
Finally, I was home. As soon as I was inside, I locked the doors and ran upstairs, slamming my bedroom door shut. *Bang! Bang! Bang!* went my bedroom door. "Who is it?" Luckily it was my mum.

Corey Pople (12)
St Dunstan's School, Glastonbury

Realisation

I remembered his last words, "This is the beginning of the end." But what exactly did he mean by that?

Only ten years later did I, myself, figure that question out. The aggravating thing was that I could no longer ask him whether I was right or not, but I was pretty sure I was.

I remembered things he'd said to me whilst growing up, I didn't think they meant anything but they were clues to the realisation of life.

I bet you're probably wondering, *who was he? Where is he?* Well, he was my brother and he killed himself...

Chantelle Aston (13)
St Dunstan's School, Glastonbury

Ouch! I Hit My Head

"Ouch!" Instead of blood there were wires hanging from the roof, lights flickered with a high-pitch squeak. Water rushed through the rusty water pipes. On the wall and floor, there were mouldy electric wires sparking. The water submerged them.

As I walked down, the power went off. It was dark. Nothing to see. I felt cobwebs around me. The lights turned off. At the end, I saw a light. Then a person. Then a group ran towards me. The red rage in their eyes was like a ruby. I started to run. I slipped, knocked out.

I woke up...

Drew Stone (13)
St Dunstan's School, Glastonbury

Lucifer's Love

They say I'm a traitor but that happens when you fall head-over-heels for someone. It happens so quickly, ripping you out of your daily routine so violently, like a bandage getting pulled off a wound.

All my emotions that I seal tightly away like a locked drawer, open, as he discovers all the keys. And now I am hand in hand with the very person that is planning to drain the life out of Earth, and I'm planning to help him.

I am in Lucifer's kingdom, sat on a throne, gripping his hand, grinning, watching the world burn.

Megan Curtis (14)
St Dunstan's School, Glastonbury

What's That?

A scream echoed outside with a loud bang. Not knowing what it was terrified me as well as me being fearful and frightened.

I jumped out of the seat with goosebumps growing up my arms. I suddenly felt cold and stiff. Then again, a scream echoed, my heartbeat quickened in seconds. My hands were shaking with tense muscles. Walking up the stairs, I started to up my pace.

In my room, I closed the door and went under the covers. I woke up and nothing was happening, nothing happened. Going downstairs, I sat down and was thankful.

Aurelia Thyer (11)
St Dunstan's School, Glastonbury

The Dark Creature

We had agreed on three meeting places, this was the last one. I drove up to the clearing, as I pulled up, headlights shone into my eyes and I heard movement. I shouted, "Mark!" There was a weird noise coming from the car, sounded like something eating.
I took out twelve rounds and loaded my handgun. I slowly walked towards the car with my gun raised. I reached the car and grabbed the handle when something dripped on my head. I looked up and saw a dark shape above me. I raised my gun when something grabbed me from behind...

Shaylah Howarth (14)
St Dunstan's School, Glastonbury

The Yellow Haze In Front Of Me

A scream echoed outside. His dark, mellow features stood out from under the streetlight, he was still, yet his emotionless face showed a brooding vision of intent. I had not seen this man before but behind the black trench coat and the unwelcoming gaze that hadn't left me, I felt a familiar feeling. A feeling of darkness, torture.

He continued to gaze, still and lifeless. I was unable to think, unable to move in a paradox of fear, until he uttered the words, "Welcome to hell," and I realised it was my father.

Anwyn Johnson (14)
St Dunstan's School, Glastonbury

Into The Darkness

A scream echoes outside. I start to run. As the twilight moon sparkles and the wind howls, I wonder what I am doing. I stop, turning back in fear. I see a shadow. The shadow asks me, "Why are you here?"
I tell him, "I don't know," but he's not there.
I lie down and doze off.
I wake up and it's back; staring at me with doubt. I get up and walk and when I turn back once again, he's not there.
As I start to walk back to my house, I wake up.
It's all just a dream.

Corey Howe (14)
St Dunstan's School, Glastonbury

One Choice

"You have one chance, choose wisely..." was the last thing he told me before he evaporated. Wondering what he meant, and what would happen after I made the choice... what if it was the wrong choice? I had no idea what to do. Should I become good or bad?

I chose the bad route, it was a mistake. They came in the night, put a bag over my head and beat me. It hurt badly. I only robbed a bank. I only took £100. They said they would do this for another ninety-nine days. On the hundredth, it would end...

Jacob Millard (13)
St Dunstan's School, Glastonbury

The Merciless Battle

They said I was a traitor because I'd dealt with more than they could live with.

It all began when we were sixteen and thought it would be fun, until men mercilessly came roaring towards us. No fear to be seen in their eyes as they came towards us.

We charged with all the fury and strength we had and fought until silence fell upon us. The wind knifed the survivors as they got up.

When we got home, we were worth nothing and meant nothing, yet I was a traitor for doing my duty.

I was nothing.

Will Porter (14)
St Dunstan's School, Glastonbury

My World

They say I'm a traitor. These voices, all of them, they hurt me. All of the 'normal' ones look at me, judging me, but they are not the ones who drove me to do this. It's the ones I hear, they don't go away and I can't see them. The people say I'm crazy, that I have 'voices' in my head. They make me laugh because voices couldn't lead me to do this. No longer will I be a vessel for them. If they exist only in my world, then I must get rid of them, with it, myself.

Youssef Louzi (13)
St Dunstan's School, Glastonbury

Trapped

A scream echoes outside, maybe this is my chance to escape. I reach to open the door but it's locked. I go towards the window. I grab the curtain and pull it back. I try to push the window open with all my power, but it won't budge. Trying to think what I can do next, I spot a chair. I grab the metal chair and chuck it at the window, then step onto the windowsill and go to escape, but suddenly the door gets kicked open with an enormous bang and then the dark figure is there.

Emillie Marshfield (14)
St Dunstan's School, Glastonbury

The Abyss

"I need to stop," I whisper to myself. The moon is wide tonight, I can hear my heart beating wildly. I go hunting in the woods at night, but tonight I fear I have awoken something.

Without instincts, I run, run until my feet can't carry me. I know it's following me but fear controls my every mood. This town has always been different, but not something like this. Tonight might be my final night, but I won't leave without a battle. *I was ready...*

Trixie Hargood (14)
St Dunstan's School, Glastonbury

Fault

They say I'm a traitor. An abomination of my own kind. I tell them to be quiet but they never stop. The taunting, the shouting, the constant pain. I'm strong, I know I am. What does it matter? If only I didn't turn my back on him, none of this would be happening. For God's sake, he was my best friend! Every night all I can think about is how the river tore him apart like a piece of tissue. I guess there is no other way and even if there were, it would be too late.

Leon Sparks (14)
St Dunstan's School, Glastonbury

The House

They said I was a traitor, they were right.
I walked over to an eerie house in the middle of the night. I thought the sun would never rise again. The moonlight shone on a piece of vine as it swished through the cold, crisp air. A leaf dropped off every time somebody took their last breath. I heard a scream... a leaf dropped off the vine. As I creaked open the door, dust swooshed around. I saw who'd screamed. I was horrified, anxious. I thought I was the next victim.

Jasmine Sheppard (11)
St Dunstan's School, Glastonbury

The Criminal's Smooth Attack

A scream echoed outside the apartment, reaching crescendo levels as he stood there at my window. He broke in, smashing my window, entering my apartment. The glass hit my face, leaving blood stains on the carpet. I quickly ran, hiding under my table. He walked over, whispering, "You're clearly unable."

I ran into my bedroom, cowering in the corner. He hit me, struck me. I knew it was my doom. I asked him, "Who are you?"

He answered, "A criminal," as he escaped, smoothly.

I grabbed my phone and dialled my friend's number.

"Michael it's me, Annie, please help me..."

Brandon MJ Evans (14)
Westfield Academy, Yeovil

The Devil Was An Angel Too

I met an angel once. Not one from renaissance art, who was all beauty and forgiveness. This angel was newly-forged iron and hellfire, deadlier than the sword in his Earth-crushing hands. He didn't have golden hair; a rusted crown adorned his treacherous head and the light shining in his eyes was a reflection of Hell, not the gates of Paradise.

Thunder was in his breath, carrying a voice that sounded like war. He looked me in the eye. In his thunderous, Earth-shattering voice, he declared, "It has begun."

Many told me he was the devil; I knew they were wrong.

Gemma Godfrey (15)
Westfield Academy, Yeovil

Thoughts Of Feeling Fake

The mist cleared and on the moss-covered gravestone, my name.

At first, I wanted to laugh, laugh at what seemed to be a sick joke, but I realised I was in denial as everything began to add up as if it was some horrific maths equation. I wanted to be sick. I wanted to reject the body I knew was fake. But I wouldn't be satisfied as the consciousness would be equally fake.

I felt the cold muzzle of a gun on my head. I wasn't supposed to know, but I still asked the silence, "Am I a clone?"

James Matthews (16)
Westfield Academy, Yeovil

The Beginning Of The End

I remembered his last words: "This is the beginning of the end." I opened the window, the cold breeze blew at me. It felt like a ghost just went into my body. I was shocked and confused about what had happened so I grabbed a blanket and ran downstairs like a mad panther was running after me. I gazed outside and saw the abandoned house. I knew I would get caught if I went there but I still wanted to go. I went.

I stayed there for ten minutes and the police came. He was right. This was the end.

Wiktoria Hajduk (12)

Westfield Academy, Yeovil

I Call Myself A Hero

They said I was a traitor. I said that was no name for a hero.
While monsters took control from above, no one was left to
help those below. It was the blood of people that kept the
city afloat. Their sweat and tears were the foundations that
the court was built upon. But the court didn't care. They
never did. They let people be slaughtered, let them suffer.
They turned a blind eye and they continued on. I couldn't do
that. I had to help. So now I was both traitor and hero.
Now I was on the run.

Megan Cait Christopher (16)
Westfield Academy, Yeovil

I Wonder Sometimes

I wonder much; so much about something, but I must not tell. I feel sick and I can't feel my legs from the cold. Steam comes out of my mouth as I take my first breath of the morning. Putting my hat and my orange scarf on, I still wonder, but I must not tell.
Walking through snow, I still wonder, but I must not tell.
I skip through the snow, then I see a black shadow, a deer, a lovely deer with brown eyes. I wonder, but I must not tell.
I will never tell, even if I must.

Eva Short (11)
Westfield Academy, Yeovil

YOUNG WRITERS INFORMATION

We hope you have enjoyed reading this book – and that you will continue to in the coming years.

If you're a young writer who enjoys reading and creative writing, or the parent of an enthusiastic poet or story writer, do visit our website **www.youngwriters.co.uk**. Here you will find free competitions, workshops and games, as well as recommended reads, a poetry glossary and our blog.

If you would like to order further copies of this book, or any of our other titles, then please give us a call or visit **www.youngwriters.co.uk**.

Young Writers
Remus House
Coltsfoot Drive
Peterborough
PE2 9BF
(01733) 890066
info@youngwriters.co.uk